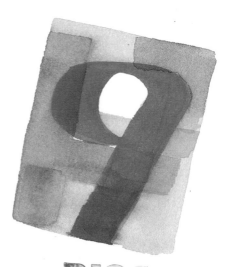

DISCARD

To my very first school, PS 87, and the little playground
that was on West 77th Street in Central Park

Dial Books for Young Readers
An imprint of Penguin Random House LLC, New York

Copyright © 2019 by David Soman

Visit us online at penguinrandomhouse.com

Printed in China
ISBN 9780525427841

1 3 5 7 9 10 8 6 4 2

Design by Jasmin Rubero
Text set in Two Fingers Bodoni

The artwork was done with watercolors, ink, and colored pencils on paper.

HOW to TWO

David Soman

Dial Books for Young Readers

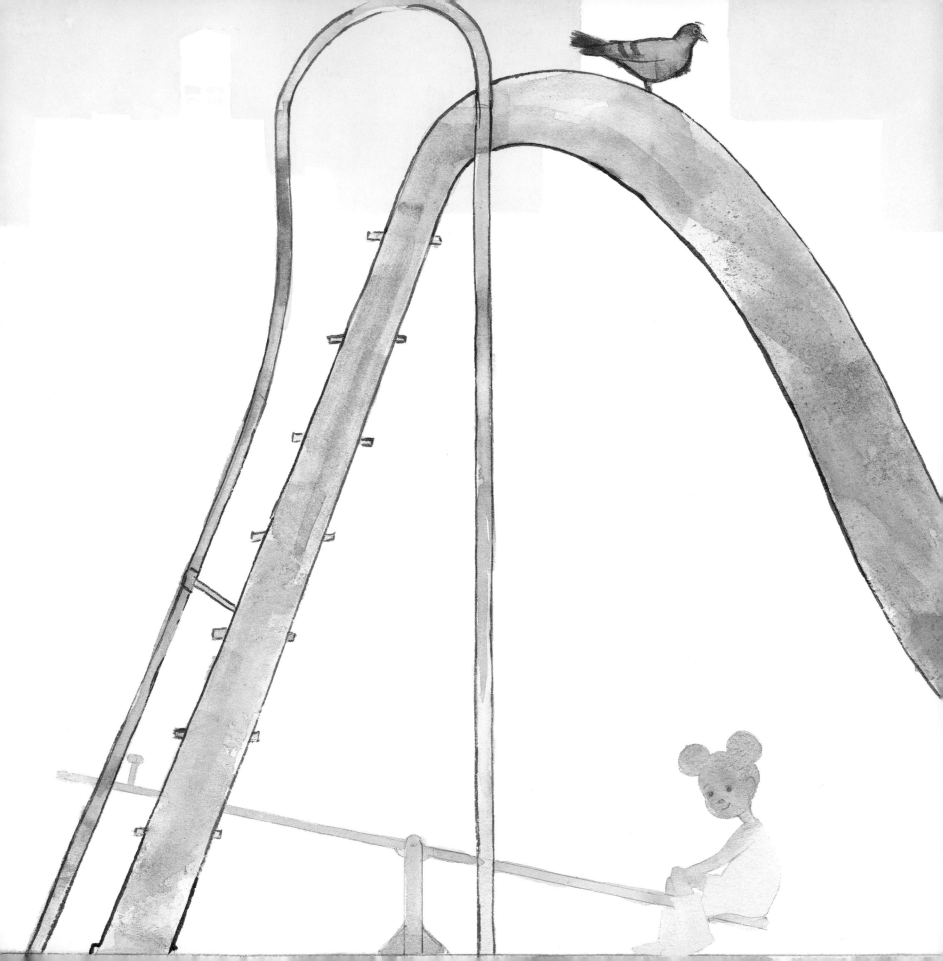

How to one.

How to two.

How to three!

How to four?

How to five!

How to . . .

six!

How to . . .

seven!

How to . . .

eight!

How to . . .

nine!

and . . .

How to ten!

How to . . .

How to one.

How to . . .

two.

Can you find these critters hidden in the book? The number is the clue!